The Hobgoblin

Stan Nicholls

 *sapling*

First published in Great Britain in 1995 by Sapling, an imprint of
Boxtree Limited, Broadwall House, 21 Broadwall, London SE1 9PL

ISBN: 0 7522 0152 2

A CIP catalogue entry for this book is available from the British
Library.

Typeset by SX Composing, Rayleigh, Essex
Printed and bound in Great Britain by Cox & Wyman, Reading,
Berkshire.

Chapter One

'I don't believe it!' Peter Parker exclaimed. 'Why do you want *me* to be your roommate?'

He was walking across the Empire State University grounds with Harry Osborn, on his way to take photographs of the inauguration ceremony to mark the start of building work on the new criminal science block.

'I know it's a little sudden,' Osborn replied, 'but it's a beautiful apartment. So how about it? Please!'

They strolled past a group of students playing Frisbee in the sunshine. Everyone seemed so relaxed.

'But we hardly know each other,' Peter said. 'Are you serious?'

'I just *have* to get out of my dad's place, but he won't pay the rent unless I have a responsible roommate. You fit the bill, Parker.'

'How am I going to afford it?' Peter asked.

'Dear old dad'll pay for everything. Only problem is, I've got to tell him today or it's no deal.'

They arrived at a roped-off area. A billboard in its centre read: FUTURE HOME OF THE FISK SCHOOL OF CRIMINOLOGY. A crowd was gathering for the ceremony. TV crews and photographers were taking up their positions.

'It's tempting,' Peter admitted, 'but I don't know what Aunt May would think about me leaving home. Let's talk after I get some pictures.'

He looked at the platform and saw his boss, J. Jonah Jameson, Publisher of the *Daily Bugle*. Next to him was Harry's father, the wealthy industrialist Norman Osborn. As Peter recalled the man's nasty reputation, the smile faded from his face.

Osborn senior took the microphone and Peter raised his camera.

'We are gathered here today to begin a great project for this university,' Norman Osborn announced.

Peter moved in closer and began snapping.

'Our new criminal science building is about to become a reality,' Osborn continued, 'thanks to the generosity of Wilson Fisk!'

The audience clapped as Fisk stepped to the microphone. He was massively built, and must have weighed at least as much as two ordinary men, but most of his bulk was muscle, not fat. His head was bald and he wore a very expensive suit. He was known to the general public as a rich businessman and do-gooder. Not so well known was the fact that in reality Fisk was the Kingpin, New York's criminal mastermind and leading mobster.

'It's a great honour for me to turn over the first load of earth,' he stated, lifting a silver shovel.

Peter felt his spider-sense tingling. There was danger nearby. But where? Then he noticed a tiny glint of metal high in the sky. In seconds the speck grew bigger. It was someone flying a bat-wing glider.

Fisk plunged the shovel into the ground, unaware of events above.

The figure on the glider could be seen quite clearly now. A cape swirled from the shoulders of his hooded costume and his face was covered by a terrifying goblin mask. He aimed a huge blaster at Wilson Fisk.

As he swooped down, the frightful figure bellowed, 'Dig, Fisk! Dig a hole wide enough for your grave!'

'Oh, boy,' Peter thought. 'Just what the world needs – another nut in a costume!' And he raced for the platform, as the goblin-masked intruder fired his weapon at Wilson Fisk.

Chapter Two

At the last possible second, Peter smashed into Fisk and knocked him aside, saving the criminal mastermind's life. The blaster beam scorched the earth, inches from where they had been.

'*That blasted kid!*' the flying attacker raged, and turned to bring the glider in for another assault.

The screaming crowd below scattered. Two policemen drew their guns but then threw themselves to the ground as the masked raider fired again. The fiery beam shot over their heads. Peter raced for a nearby

7

university building.

Fisk, was hustled to his limousine by security guards. He pointed to the sky and growled, 'I want to know who that madman is!' With that, his white limo sped away.

The raider swooped low to survey the damage. Then he saw a figure swinging towards him on a thin strand of webbing

'*Spider-Man!*' he gasped.

'Sorry, gruesome, you're too late for Hallowe'en!'

'The name's Hobgoblin!' the costumed brigand yelled back. 'And *you're* right on time . . . for your funeral!'

He shot a bolt of energy that cut

through Spider-Man's web, but Spidey made it to a nearby roof. He immediately used his web-shooter to send a line to the top of a taller building and swung up to it. Within seconds, Hobgoblin's glider arrived beside him.

'Why are you after Fisk?' Spider-Man demanded.

'Oh, nothing personal,' Hobgoblin replied sarcastically.

'Well,' said Spider-Man, '*this* is!' and dived at him. But he missed.

Hobgoblin shrieked with laughter.

Twisting in the air, Spider-Man shot another web. Hobgoblin simply flew into it and sliced it apart with the sharp edge of his glider's wing.

'What agility!' Spider-Man thought. 'He's out-thinking me every step of the way!'

He managed to hook the corner of an adjoining building with his web. The glider returned, zooming overhead, and Spider-Man lurched upward, catching hold of its wing.

Hobgoblin made the craft climb as Spider-Man hung on for dear life. They headed straight for a Jumbo Jet.

'Enjoying the flight?' Hobgoblin cackled.

The jet was directly ahead.

'Nah,' said Spider-Man. 'I've seen the in-flight movie. I'm getting out of here.' And with that, he let go.

Hobgoblin swerved, narrowly missing the airliner. Spider-Man plummeted downwards. Falling past the nearest skyscraper, he aimed his web-shooter.

Thwipp!

'Oh, no!' he thought to himself, 'I'm out of web-fluid!'

He struck the angled roof of an adjacent building and, out of control, slid down the slope and over the edge. The front of the building was covered in scaffolding and cloth sheeting. Spider-Man plunged into one of the sheets and his foot became entangled. For a moment his fall was halted, but then the side of the sheet tore away and he fell again.

Headfirst, he dropped towards an iron fence topped by wickedly sharp spikes. Suddenly the sheeting around his ankle pulled taut and he yanked to a stop just inches above them – a little too close for comfort!

Hanging upside-down, he saw the Hobgoblin flying away. 'How do I *find* all these nutcases?' he panted.

Norman Osborn had just arrived in his laboratory at the Oscorp building when Hobgoblin flew in through an open skylight.

Osborn glared and said, 'You've failed me – *miserably*.'

'No!' Hobgoblin sneered. '*You* failed to tell *me* Spider-Man would get involved! Now the price for removing Fisk goes up.'

'No way!'

'Why do you want to take him out anyway?' Hobgoblin asked.

'None of your business! You're fired!' He pointed at the wing glider. 'And leave me *that*.'

'Don't talk to me like I'm some punk!'

The Hobgoblin stared at Osborn in disbelief, then levelled his blaster at the shady business man.

'Before I gave you the wing and weapons you *were* just a punk. A crook in a Hallowe'en mask! Don't forget, I know your real identity. If anything happens to me, it comes out!'

Hobgoblin soared up to the skylight. 'You *owe* me, Osborn! And I'm taking the wing as down-payment!' His mad laughter echoed behind him.

Chapter Three

' . . . *A young* Bugle *photographer, Peter Parker, pushed Fisk out of harm's way . . .*' the TV announcer explained.

Peter and Aunt May were sitting in the living room watching the news over dinner.

'Good gracious, Peter, you could have been *hurt*,' Aunt May said. 'If I'm to sleep peacefully at night when you're living on your own, you must promise to stop taking these risks.'

'I won't move out if you don't want me to,' Peter replied.

'No, no. It's something young

people have to do.'

He smiled. 'I knew you'd understand.' Then his face grew more serious and he added, 'But I want you to know that no matter where I go, I'll always be here if you need me.'

'Well, thank you, dear.' She gathered up the dishes. 'Ready for dessert?'

'Sure!'

Aunt May quickly walked into the kitchen and as soon as she was out of sight her smile vanished. Looking suddenly very lost and alone, she sadly wiped a tear from her eye.

Later that evening, suitcase in

hand, Peter arrived at his new apartment. There was a party going on inside and when Harry answered the door, loud music blasted out.

'Hey, Pete! You almost missed our big house-warming!'

Peter was amazed at the size of the penthouse. 'It's *incredible!* When do I get to thank your dad?'

Harry frowned. 'Who knows? He hasn't been here yet. Too busy with his precious work at Oscorp. . . . Look, I've got to take care of the guests.'

He disappeared into the crowd of dancing and chattering people, but at that point Peter's friend Mary Jane Watson came over.

'Peter!' she exclaimed. 'What a *beautiful* place.'

He nodded, grinning, and went to his room to dump the suitcase. The view from the enormous windows was spectacular.

'Moving out could be the best thing I ever did,' he thought.

Across town, Hobgoblin flew through the hole he'd cut high in the side of Fisk's office building and searched it. He found nothing, except the secret elevator which would whisk him away to the very nerve centre of the Kingpin's operations. Hobgoblin stepped inside. A few moments later, the doors opened to a gigantic chamber full of electronic gadgets. And a dozen heavily armed men.

The Kingpin appeared. 'How convenient! Welcome!'

Hobgoblin threw back his head and laughed fearlessly. 'So it really exists! Crime Central, the HQ controlling most of the crime on this planet! I thought it was a myth.'

'It was bold of you to come here,' Kingpin said. 'Give me one good reason why I shouldn't have you disposed of immediately.'

'Aren't you curious about who ordered the hit on you?' Hobgoblin asked, looking round in admiration.

'And what do you want in return?'

'Money! And a place in your organization.' He smiled knowingly.

'That could be arranged. But first, tell me the name.'

'Norman Osborn.'

'*Osborn!*' The Kingpin smashed his fist on the desk. 'Well, I'll have to teach him a lesson!' He gazed at his strange visitor. 'At the same time, I'll test your loyalty to me. First, we shall equip you with a more fearsome arsenal . . .'

Chapter Four

Next morning, the apartment was in a terrible mess. Peter wandered around groggily, picking his way through spilt drinks, dirty dishes and scattered CDs.

The telephone rang. 'Yes? *What?*' He slammed down the receiver and called out to Harry.

His new roommate staggered out of his bedroom, yawning. 'What's all the racket?'

'My Aunt May's on her way up! And look at the state of this place!'

As they heard the doorbell, Peter's spider-sense tingled. 'That's odd,' he thought. 'I wonder why it should go off just as Aunt May arrives.'

He opened the door and his aunt looked around in horror. 'Peter? What on *earth* – ?'

But she never finished the sentence, for at that very moment there was an insane chuckle and a gas bomb rolled in through the open balcony window, exploding in a choking green cloud. Peter and Aunt May gaped as Hobgoblin leapt into the room.

Recognizing Peter, he exclaimed, '*You!* Perfect! Two birds with one stone!'

He whipped out a Pumpkin bomb from his pouch and threw it at them. Peter did his best to shield Aunt May, but it was a hopeless task. There was a loud blast, then smoke and dust filled the room and plaster showered from the ceiling. As he went down, Peter heard Harry's terrified scream.

When the air cleared some time later Peter was on the floor, surrounded by wrecked furniture. He got to his feet shakily and called, 'Aunt May? Harry?'

There was a groan. He found Aunt May stretched out by the door, moaning softly.

'Aunt May! Can you hear me? *Aunt May!*'

Scrabbling wildly through the debris, he finally located the telephone and frantically punched the emergency number. 'I need an ambulance! Fast!'

He sat stunned for a while, gazing down at Aunt May. 'Why do the people I care about always get hurt when I'm just trying to do the right thing?' he whispered. 'If you don't pull through, I'll never be able to live with myself.'

Hobgoblin strode out of the elevator into Crime Central. Along with him he dragged Harry, tied up and looking very scared.

The Kingpin stepped forward. 'I am pleased, Hobgoblin. Very pleased.' He jabbed his thumb at a transparent plastic cylinder hanging from the ceiling. 'Now, put *him* in the cell,' he ordered.

When Harry was locked in his suspended prison, he blurted out, 'What do you want from me?'

'Your dad's loaded,' Hobgoblin told him. 'Work it out for yourself.' He turned to the Kingpin. 'Now, about that bonus –'

'All in good time.'

'Hey, I earned it! Pay up!'

'You'll be paid when I say so! You work for *me* now. Don't forget that.'

The video-phone on Norman Osborn's desk flashed. He hit the *answer* key and the Kingpin's face appeared on the screen.

'Ah, Norman. Glad to see you so hard at work.'

'What do you want, Fisk? I'm busy.'

'Too busy to talk about your son?'

The screen showed Harry in his plastic cell, clearly terrified.

'What have you done with my son?' Osborn demanded.

'This is what happens when someone tries to double-cross me,' the Kingpin replied.

Hobgoblin's image filled the video-phone monitor. He waved and laughed.

'I was surprised when you sent Hobgoblin after me,' the Kingpin continued. 'I didn't know you wanted to end my silent partnership in Oscorp. But so be it. All I want now are your inventions.'

'But . . . they're my life's work! I'll be ruined!'

'You have twenty-four hours to sign them over to me. Your life's work . . . or your son!'

The screen went back.

Chapter Five

A nurse tended Aunt May as Peter angrily paced the hospital room like a caged animal.

'That giggling piece of dirt,' he muttered, 'I'll rip his – '

'Peter?'

He spun round to find Mary Jane at the door, a bunch of flowers in her hand. 'I was worried,' she said. 'I had to come.'

'Thanks.' He paused, then asked, 'Any word from the police about Harry?'

She shook her head, and together they looked at Aunt May's still form.

'This is all my fault,' Peter sighed.

'No, it isn't. Hobgoblin's a lunatic, attacking people at random.'

'Not at random. He wanted *me*.'

'Or did he?' he thought. 'How could he know I lived there? And didn't he say something about two birds with one stone?'

Suddenly making his mind up, he headed for the door. 'I've got to go out for a while. Can you stay with Aunt May?'

Mary Jane looked startled. 'Sure. But where – ?'

He'd gone before she could finish.

*

In his laboratory at Oscorp, Norman Osborn was also pacing. His thoughts were broken when, once more, Hobgoblin flew in through the skylight.

'Osborn! We've got to talk!'

'*Talk?* You kidnapped my son!' Osborn lunged at him, but Hobgoblin darted out of the way.

'I had to do it to stay alive! The Kingpin's a double-crossing snake!'

'And you're a liar!'

'This time I'm telling the truth,' Hobgoblin insisted, 'and I've got a plan. We can get Fisk together.'

'What do you mean?'

'Let *me* rescue Harry. That way, you'll have your company *and* your son.'

Hobgoblin prepares to fire a huge blaster at Wilson Fisk from his bat-winged glider.

Spider-Man swings through the air armed with his web-shooters in his chase after Hobgoblin.

Kingpin uses Hobgoblin for his own purposes, but is the cloaked villain to be trusted . . .

Hobgoblin demonstrates the power of his special weapons.

Osborn should learn not to do business with the double-crossing Hobgoblin!

Kingpin calls in the guards when Hobgoblin reveals his plans to take over Crime Central.

Spider-Man is on the right track . . .

Spider-Man saves Harry from Hobgoblin's 'evil clutches with not a minute to spare.

'What's in it for you?'

'I want the Kingpin,' he said darkly. 'But to get back into his HQ I need a better weapon.'

'I've already given you all I have!'

'C'mon, Norm! You geniuses always have another one on the drawing board.'

Osborn sighed and pressed a button on the control panel beside him. A section of the wall slid back to reveal a much larger bat-wing glider.

'It goes twice as high and four times as fast as your old glider,' he explained. 'It's got missiles, and there's even remote control.'

Hobgoblin caught the remote-control device Osborn tossed to him and whistled in appreciation. At which point the door exploded open.

Spider-Man strode into the room. 'New wing, same jerk!' he hissed.

Osborn backed away in shock.

'What a great chance to test my wonderful new toy!' Hobgoblin yelled gleefully, and he jumped on the glider and rose towards the skylight.

Spider-Man fired a web-line at the wing and was immediately dragged after him. They shot through the skylight together at a tremendous rate.

'Let's see what this baby can

do!' Hobgoblin shouted as he increased speed.

He rolled the glider over, flipping it in the air, with Spider-Man helplessly corkscrewing along behind. Then he headed for a radio aerial on top of a skyscraper. Swerving, he flew a complete loop around it. Spider-Man's webbing wrapped around the aerial, went suddenly taut . . . and then snapped.

He fell.

Hobgoblin looked down. 'Now for a couple of missiles!' he bellowed, stamping a foot pedal.

Chapter Six

Spider-Man tumbled downwards, the twin missiles in hot pursuit.

As the ground loomed closer he shot out a web-line. It attached to the ledge of a high building and yanked him to a sudden stop. The missiles zapped overhead and flew off into the night sky.

Spider-Man clambered to the roof and stared at the huge advertising billboard on it. Up above, Hobgoblin fired razor discs, viciously sharp circular blades with saw teeth, and they hammered into the billboard like machine-gun fire, shredding it as

Spider-Man dived for cover.

Then Hobgoblin aimed the wing glider straight at him. Spider-Man tried to dodge, but it was no good. The glider hit him square in the chest, and with a grunt he was pulled off the building, hanging on to the craft grimly.

'How about a tour of the city?' Hobgoblin jeered.

They nosedived to the streets and soared just above them at tremendous speed. The glider veered dangerously from side to side, and after a while Spider-Man knew he just couldn't hold on any longer. At the end of the street there was a house under construction and as they flew past he jumped for an open window.

But as he leapt he saw the two missiles that had been fired earlier coming after him.

'*Oh, no!* They must be locked on me!'

He flipped into the window and hit the floor, and still the missiles homed in.

Hobgoblin flew up and away. 'So long, sucker!' he cackled.

Inside, Spider-Man rolled to his feet and desperately looked for an escape route. The missiles would find him in seconds. He spotted another window at the back of the house and made a dash for it. He smashed through just as the missiles struck.

A gigantic explosion utterly destroyed the house.

Spider-Man picked himself up from the pavement as the dust settled. 'Where are those sky-scrapers when you need 'em?' he complained. 'Can't get *airborne . . .*'

The roar of an engine could be heard above. He turned. Hob-goblin was coming in fast, strafing the street with a laser Gatling gun. People scattered wildly. Spider-Man lunged to one side.

Hobgoblin swerved and re-turned, coming in low and fast.

As Spider-Man ran for cover, a razor disc sliced a nearby lamp-post in two. He changed direction and threw himself under a parked minibus. There was a drain grating beneath it.

'Think you're smart, Spider-Man?' Hobgoblin roared. 'Try *this*!'

He unleashed another missile, which streaked towards the minibus, blowing it to pieces.

'Happy trails!' Hobgoblin yelled as he flew into the night.

Further along the street, beyond the burning wreck, a man-hole cover opened. Spider-Man's head popped out of the sewer.

Police sirens could be heard as he watched Hobgoblin's glider disappearing.

'You don't get rid of me *that* easily,' he promised. 'Not after what you did to Aunt May.'

Chapter Seven

In his laboratory, Norman Osborn was watching TV.

'. . . *Harry Osborn was kidnapped by a masked man calling himself Hobgoblin,*' the newscaster said. '*Osborn's father, industrialist Norman, has refused to comment on –*'

At that moment a shadow fell across Osborn and he whirled around. Spider-Man faced him.

'What did Hobgoblin want from you?' he demanded.

'You can't just come in here and –'

'What did he *want*?' Spider-Man

repeated menacingly.

'I can't tell you. It . . . it's personal.'

Spider-Man grabbed the scruff of Osborn's shirt and lifted him off the ground. 'You *better* tell me. It's personal for me, too.'

'Look, it's all been taken care of.'

Spider-Man let him down and said, 'Don't tell me you made a *deal* with that madman?'

Osborn looked embarrassed.

'You trusted Hobgoblin!' Spider-Man exclaimed with disbelief.

'I had to! I could lose my company, my inventions . . . everything!'

'What about your son?'

'I said *everything*. Look, don't judge me. I know what I'm doing. This'll all be over by midnight.'

'Midnight, eh? Then expect to see me one minute after . . . just to make sure!'

Spider-Man headed for the door, leaving Osborn to sink slowly back into his chair.

'It's time I got paid,' Hobgoblin told the Kingpin.

They sat opposite each other in Crime Central. There was no one else in the vast chamber.

'I've got something to show you first,' the Kingpin said, activating a monitor.

A recording of Hobgoblin and

Norman Osborn came on the screen.

'When someone works for me,' the Kingpin growled, 'I expect complete loyalty. Not *treachery*!'

Hobgoblin stood and walked to his wing glider. 'I was getting what I could for myself, Fisk. It's good business.'

The Kingpin pointed at the screen. 'You betrayed me, and I will not tolerate that. Guards, terminate him!'

Dozens of armed men appeared from the shadows.

'*No!*' Hobgoblin raged, swiftly reaching into his pouch.

He produced a handful of pumpkin bombs and tossed them

at the guards. Smoke, gas and shrapnel exploded in all directions. In the chaos, Hobgoblin shot upwards on his glider.

'He must not get away!' the Kingpin bellowed, and his men began firing their weapons.

Hobgoblin's glider turned sharply and he swooped down on them, hurling more bombs and opening up with the laser Gatling. Several guards fell and others, losing their nerve, dashed for the elevator and stairs in blind panic.

Then Hobgoblin saw the Kingpin running for an alcove in the wall. He sped after him and lobbed a bomb. It detonated loudly. The floor trembled and a sheet of flame went up. Plaster rained from the ceiling and the alcove was buried in rubble.

'Well, what do you know?' Hobgoblin grinned. 'I finally got him!'

He looked around the now deserted chamber. The smoke and dust were starting to clear.

'It's a little worse for wear,' he decided, 'but the important thing is . . . it's mine.' He rocked with evil, hysterical laughter. 'Crime Central is mine! *All mine!*'

Chapter Eight

Hobgoblin stood before a bank of screens in Crime Central, gleefully hitting buttons.

'Every inch of optical fibre, every byte of information . . . all mine!'

He pressed a button that brought Harry's transparent cell down from the ceiling and, wrenching open the door, dragged him out.

'My father paid the ransom?' Harry said hopefully. 'I'm free to go?'

'Free?' Hobgoblin replied. 'Nothing with me is ever *free*!

You're mine now. And so is all this!' Pushing Harry to the control console, he continued, 'See? Instant contact with any place on Earth.' His fingers played across a keyboard. Monitors lit up and showed crimes in progress. There were car chases, shoot-outs, kidnappings and robberies. 'But I don't just observe,' Hobgoblin went on, 'I *control* the information. And the better I control it, the more money I make.' He indicated the chamber with a sweep of his hand. 'I have everything here: power, water, security – I can stay for ever.'

'Then what do you want from my father?' Harry asked.

'Revenge. And now that I have you, I'm going to get it!'

The video-phone rang in Norman Osborn's lab. He punched *answer* and Hobgoblin's face appeared.

'Evening, Osborn!'

'You were supposed to come back here. What went wrong?'

'Nothing. Your wing's a marvel. It helped me destroy the Kingpin, just like you wanted from the start.'

'Then why aren't you here?'

'I've rethought our deal, Osborn. Now I've got Kingpin's crime empire, I want Oscorp, too. All of it!'

'Why, you . . . Remember, I know your true identity. I'll –'

Hobgoblin jerked his son into view.

'Harry!' Osborn gasped.

'This town has a new Kingpin,' Hobgoblin told him. '*Me!*'

Then the screen blanked out.

'Come back!' Osborn raged. 'You filthy, rotten, lying –'

'I believe the word is *traitor.*'

He spun around. The Kingpin was behind him.

Osborn whispered, 'But he said you were –'

'He was wrong. And you're the fool for bringing this down on yourself.'

'It was because of you! Bleeding my company dry! You left me no choice.'

'Let's not squabble. I suggest we combine our forces to eliminate Hobgoblin.'

'How?'

'There's a secret tunnel to my headquarters,' the Kingpin explained. 'I used it to escape. All I need from *you* is a weapon to combat that wing.'

'A weapon?' Osborn said thoughtfully. 'I just might have something. Or perhaps I should say some*one* . . .'

'I don't know why I'm trusting you, Osborn,' Spider-Man said.

'We both want the Hobgoblin, don't we?'

'Oh, I want him all right.'

It was after midnight. They were outside an old, half-destroyed pumping station by the river.

Osborn pointed into the ruins. 'There's a tunnel in there.'

'You better not be playing games,' Spider-Man warned him, 'because I know where to find you.' With that, he moved off into the darkness.

After he'd gone, a white limousine pulled up. Osborn got in. 'He's on his way,' he reported.

The Kingpin smiled. 'A brilliant idea! Using one of our enemies to fight the other. This should be quite a show!'

Chapter Nine

Spider-Man kicked down a metal door leading to the tunnel. It was pitch black and rats scurried around him. He thought of Aunt May in her hospital bed, then plunged into the gloom.

Coming to an elevator, he pressed its only button and was carried upwards. When the doors opened, he faced a wooden panel. Easing it aside, he gazed into Crime Central.

Hobgoblin was sitting there, with his back to him.

Spider-Man didn't know it, but he was looking through the secret doorway the Kingpin had used to escape. He saw Hobgoblin's wing glider a few feet away and immediately shot a glob of thick web at it.

Hobgoblin heard the sound and turned, but couldn't see his foe. 'Spider-Man? How did – ? Never mind. Let me give you a *proper* greeting!' And with that he tossed a smoke grenade.

Using the cloud for cover, Hobgoblin dashed to the glider, but couldn't budge it.

Spider-Man jumped from the alcove. 'Stuck? How about a kick-start?'

He launched himself at Hobgoblin feet first, striking him in the chest. The villain hit the ground. Still on his back, he pulled a handful of razor-winged bats from his belt and hurled them.

Nimbly, Spider-Man dodged the boomerang-like weapons. One hit a cable, releasing a dazzling shower of sparks. As Spidey dived away, Hobgoblin made for the glider again.

'All flights have been cancelled!' Spider-Man yelled, firing a web.

Hobgoblin used a razor-wing to cut the webbing away. Then he flung a bomb.

The explosion propelled Spider-Man into a wall, stunning him. A smoke grenade followed and he lost sight of the costumed hit-man.

'Get out here now!' Spider-Man demanded furiously. 'Come and face me!'

Suddenly, Hobgoblin shot from the cloud on his glider. 'Careful what you wish for!' he mocked, pitching another pumpkin bomb.

But Spider-Man caught it in a spray of webbing and slung it straight back. The bomb blew up midway between them, knocking Spidey off his feet and Hobgoblin out of the air. A number of fires immediately started to blaze.

'It's all ruined!' Hobgoblin raged as he saw the damage. 'I've lost everything!'

'You've still got your life,' Spider-Man replied. 'For the moment.' He advanced and added, 'Where's Harry Osborn?'

Hobgoblin snatched a razor sharp bat-wing from his belt. 'You want him? You got him!' He lobbed the wing up at the cable holding Harry's cell. It snapped.

Spider-Man dashed forward and broke the plunging cell's fall. Landing on its side, the door sprang open and Harry tumbled out unconscious.

In the meantime, Hobgoblin had vanished.

Lifting his friend, Spider-Man carried him through the smoke and flames to the secret elevator.

As soon as they'd gone, the Kingpin entered through another secret doorway. He hurried to the console and began pressing buttons. Water gushed from the ceiling, putting out the fires.

'It worked, exactly as planned,' he muttered to himself. He took in the surrounding destruction. 'I'll have to rebuild this place. But I'll make it bigger and better than before.' A smile twisted his lips. 'The main thing is, Crime Central is mine again!'

Chapter Ten

Spider-Man carried Harry into Norman Osborn's lab and laid him on a couch.

Osborn rushed to them. 'What's wrong with him?'

'He took a fall,' Spider-Man said. 'He'll be OK.'

'And Hobgoblin?'

'Gone.'

Osborn smiled. 'Then it's over.'

'It's *not* over,' Spider-Man retorted. 'I've got a lot of questions and I think you know the answers.'

'That wasn't part of our deal.'

Spider-Man grabbed Osborn by his shoulders. 'Still playing games, eh? Like the games you played with Hobgoblin, and with your son's life!'

'Let go! You think I don't care about Harry? Well, I do.' He stared at his son. 'My work was always everything to me, and I guess I neglected him. But that doesn't mean I don't care. Maybe I made the wrong choices . . .'

Harry groaned and began to come round.

Suddenly Spider-Man looked up. His spider-sense was tingling and, sure enough, there was Hobgoblin leering at them from the skylight.

'It's pay-back time, Osborn!' he screeched, dropping a bomb.

The deafening explosion wrecked the lab. In the confusion a

large wooden beam gave way and fell towards Harry. Too weak to move, he weakly yelled, '*No-o-o-o!*'

His father leapt forward to shield his body and the beam crashed down on to his back.

Spider-Man rushed over and tore the beam away. 'You OK?' he asked.

'Dad?' Harry whispered.

Norman Osborn blinked, coughed and said, 'We're OK . . .'

'Guess he finally made the right choice,' Spider-Man said quietly.

He shot a web at the skylight and hauled himself to the roof.

Hobgoblin floated in the air nearby. 'So you're here too,' he cackled. 'How very convenient!'

'Yeah . . . for me.'

Spider-Man swung at him and Hobgoblin launched a barrage of missiles. Spidey dodged and weaved, and the missiles shot past him. One struck a distant fuel tank, which erupted into flames.

Meanwhile, Spider-Man had landed on the side of a tall factory chimney. Out of missiles, Hobgoblin flew straight at him and Spidey started to climb. He reached the top of the chimney as his enemy zoomed in for the attack. Hobgoblin circled, trying to clip him with his wing, but Spider-Man was too agile to be caught.

Finally, Hobgoblin went into a steep dive, shouting, 'Let's get this over with!'

At the very last second, Spider-Man jumped *into* the chimney.

Hobgoblin's wing clipped the top of it and he lost control. The glider spun into the smoke from the burning fuel tank. Then he zigzagged out of the cloud and plunged into the river beyond.

Spider-Man's head poked out of the chimney. '*That* was for Aunt May,' he said grimly. He knew that the Hobgoblin was a cunning force, and that he would no doubt return soon – but, for the time being, Spider-Man had won.

'Where have you *been?*' Mary Jane asked Peter.

'I . . . I had to take care of

something. How is she?'

'Still the same.'

They gazed at Aunt May's silent face.

Slowly, her eyelids fluttered. 'Peter?' she whispered.

He took her hand. 'We were so worried about you.'

'It was such a shock,' Aunt May said.

'Don't worry, Hobgoblin's gone now.'

'Who's talking about *him*?' she replied. 'It was your apartment! I've never *seen* such a mess. I don't think you're ready to live on your own yet.'

Peter smiled. 'I think you're right,' he agreed.